בס"ד
לד׳ הארץ ומלואה

This book belongs to:

Hachai

Please read it to me!

I Go to Sleep

לע״נ אורי חיים יוסף ע״ה בן משה הלוי נ״י
In memory of my dear nephew, a"h, who was extraordinary in his lifetime.
With tremendous bitachon, he lived each day b'simcha despite his challenges.
May his zechus bring his family brocha. R. B.

First Edition – Cheshvan 5779 / October 2018
Copyright © 2018 by HACHAI PUBLISHING
ALL RIGHTS RESERVED

Editor: Devorah Leah Rosenfeld
Managing Editor: Yossi Leverton
Layout: Moshe Cohen

ISBN: 978-1-945560-11-8
LCCN: 2018942031

Hachai Publishing
Brooklyn, New York
Tel: 718-633-0100
Fax: 718-633-0103
info@hachai.com
www.hachai.com

Printed in China

Glossary

Hashem	G-d
Mitzvos	Commandments, good deeds
Negel vasser	Ritual hand washing
Sh'ma Yisroel	The 'Hear O Israel' Prayer

I Go to
Sleep

written and illustrated by
Rikki Benenfeld

Today was wonderful and fun,
Supper's over – playtime's done.

At the end of this busy day,

It's time to put my things away.

In the bath, I wash and scrub,
And play with bubbles in the tub.

My teeth are next – I never rush,
Making sure to floss and brush.

I fill my negel vasser cup,

Ready for when I wake up.

On go pajamas – one, two, three,
I'm ready for bed as fast as can be!

**Now it's time to listen and look,
And hear a favorite bedtime book.**

A goodnight kiss and a great big hug,
Make me feel all warm and snug.

I cover my eyes and say Sh'ma with care,
Hashem is One. He's everywhere!

He's always watching over me,
I'll stay in bed all night – you'll see!

My parents tuck me in just right,

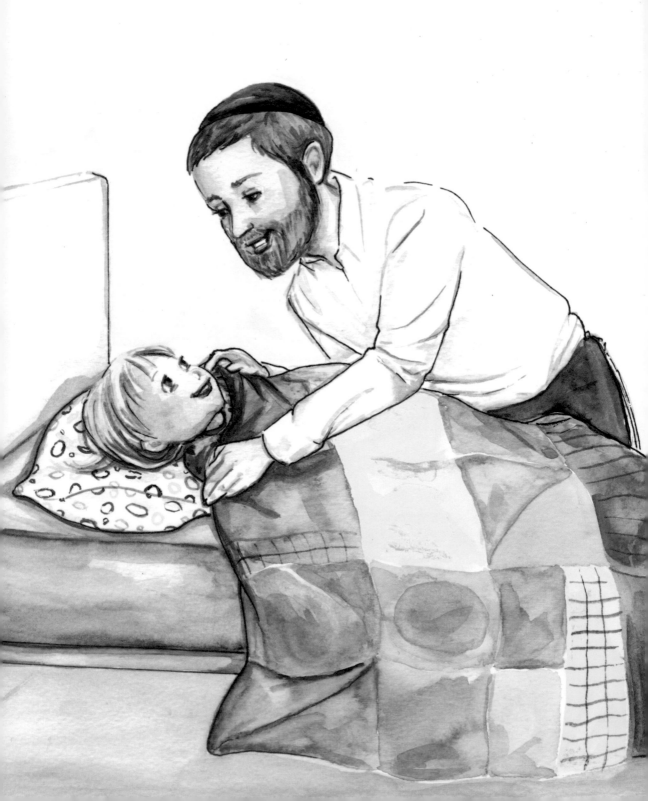

"I love you.
Good night, good night!"

I rest on my pillow and think for a while
About mitzvos I did to make Hashem smile.

With happy thoughts to dream about,
I breathe slowly, in and out.

Not a sound, not a peep,

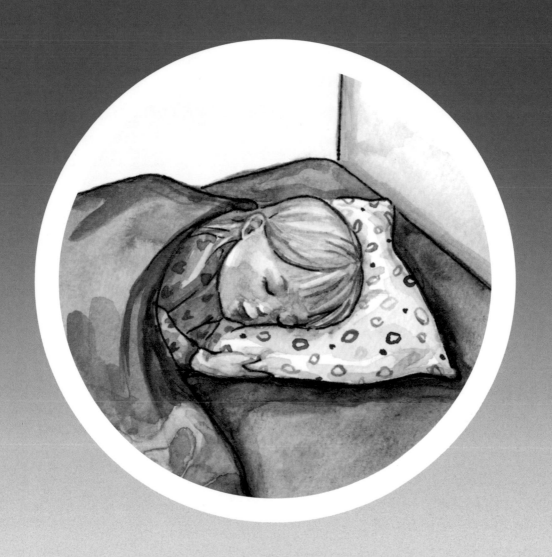

Quietly, I go to sleep.

Prepare your child for life's experiences with:

The Toddler Experience Series

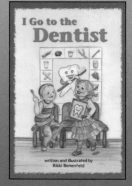

Featuring mitzvah opportunities, politeness, hygiene, safety and appropriate behavior in every situation!